# Agnes of Rome
## A Novella

## Catherine Brigden

# DEDICATION

This book is dedicated to all Christian martyrs of the past and present for their courage to stand against those who would try to stop the spread of the Gospel of Jesus Christ.

# CONTENTS

# ACKNOWLEDGMENTS

Many thanks to my husband Allen and the rest of my family for their support in completing this project. I especially thank my parents for giving me the resources to be able to study in the Rome Semester at the University of Dallas which helped to inspire this story. Additional credit is given to works which helped me make this work as historically accurate as possible and provide quotes of scripture in everyday language. They can be found in the bibliography at the end of this book. Thanks to all people who have guided me on my Christian journey. Other recognition goes to members of the Barnard Memorial United Methodist Church of Holdenville, Oklahoma for encouraging me to finish and for their constructive criticism.

# 1

Some people might say that I had a death wish. They might say I didn't love life or have hope for the future. On the contrary, I love my life still. I am with my true love, Jesus, and I want to tell you my story.

I was born in Rome on January 28, A.D. 292 to Christian parents. My father's name was Paulus Clodius Crescentianus. My mother was Segunda, since she was the second daughter of her father. Father was a wealthy landowner, and my family had much influence in the local politics of Rome. I consider myself blessed to have grown up in a comfortable home where I could learn of the love of Jesus Christ.

This story begins when I was only ten years of age. As was traditional for girls my age, and class; I was fortunate to be educated by a Greek tutor. His name was Hector. He was a Christian too. He taught me to read and write in Latin and Greek. I enjoyed reading the works of Plato and learning about the history of the great empire I live in. I felt as if I knew Paul of Tarsus personally from his letters to the Church. I also learned of the love and sacrifice of Jesus Christ from the Gospel of Mark.

When I was born, it was reasonably safe to be a Christian. Septimus Severus had been out of power for over a half century, and Rome had become tolerant of us again. We built our churches and held meetings every Sunday. Worship was wonderful. I would listen to the stories of how Jesus would turn worldly thinking upside down.

Many of my friends from childhood were pagan. They would go with their parents to make sacrifices to spirits and gods that may or may not exist. They had gods for everything. They had shrines in their homes with idols that represented their deceased family members and prayed to them as if they were gods as well. Spirits and fate controlled everything, and they must be appeased, usually with animal sacrifice. Even the emperor was a god. I never really figured that one out.

Sometimes my friends' parents wouldn't let me play with them anymore because they feared that I was dangerous. My family did not worship the gods of the State. We basically ignored them. Most Romans believed that if Roman citizens did not worship the gods properly on the proper days in the proper manner, the gods would become angry and the Roman State would end. They weren't far from the truth. The only problem was that they didn't realize which God they had angered.

On Holy Saturday in my tenth year, I was confirmed into the Church. Since I was born to Christian parents, I was baptized as a baby. Converts to the Church needed to be educated fully in our ways before they were able to receive the sacraments, for their safety and ours. One never knew when the emperor might change his mind about us. It was a great honor that the bishop of Rome presided at my entry into the Church. I wanted to be a pure example of womanhood. During Holy Week much of my time was spent in contemplation of the sacrifice that Jesus made for humanity. I also remembered some of Paul's writings about purity. I took the name of Agnes which means "pure".

The Holy Spirit had come upon me many times during worship and during prayer. However, when the bishop laid his hands upon me, a rush of wind surged through my body. He touched every part of my being. I could feel His love. It was at that moment that I was convinced that I would love no other man. Jesus is mine. He died for me, and I was willing to die for Him.

During the next year I spent more time with Hector and my studies. My parents believed that being well educated would make me a good match for a young man who may want to court and eventually marry me. I could understand that, especially if I was to marry the son of a nobleman. Marriage was expected of all young women in Roman society. I could be a good asset to my husband if I was well educated.

One afternoon my mother called me to her chambers. "Agnes, there are several things we need to discuss."

I didn't have any idea what she would need to discuss with me. "Have I disappointed you in some way, Mother? Am I fulfilling my duties the way that you wish?"

"Oh, yes, my dear. You misunderstand me. You are nearing the age of when young men will be calling upon you as suitors for marriage. We need to address issues and questions that you may have on this matter."

"What do you mean?"

"Well, your body will be changing quite dramatically in the next few months or years, and I want you to be prepared for what will happen. Also, young men are going to notice some of these changes in you, and you need to be aware of what these men are seeing, so you can guard your honor for the man you will eventually marry."

"What is going to happen?"

"You may have seen it in some of your friends. You will begin to blossom in your bosom, and you will begin to show more curves around your hips and thighs and begin to bleed from your womb once a month. You will also start to notice young men in a different way as well."

"I don't think I am going to like the bleeding part."

My mother chuckled, "Well, it isn't always the most pleasant experience, but it is a gift from God. He created you as a woman and has gifted you with the ability to bear children. Your body will be going through the changes that are necessary for you to be able to have them."

"What if I don't want to have children?"

"You will have to take that issue up with your husband. However, being a noble daughter, Rome expects you to marry and bear her many sons."

"What does Jesus expect me to do?"

"He expects you to follow his call. I expect you to follow his call as well. I am only telling you these things so that you will know what to expect. It is up to you to follow God's will for your life and make choices based upon that."

"That is a lot of responsibility. I'm not old enough to make those kinds of decisions."

"Yes, it is much responsibility, but it is no more responsibility than what God gave to Adam and Eve when He told them not to eat from the tree of knowledge of good and evil. They chose to eat of that fruit rather than eat of the fruit from the tree of life. I hope you choose to follow God's will. I believe that He will lead you to the right path. It will be up to you to follow it or not."

My mother gave me a kiss on the forehead and left me alone with my thoughts. What was going on? Me like boys? She has got to be out of her mind. I was perfectly happy with my studies of history and Jesus. I had no desire to ever get married, at least right now.

## 2

There was much political turmoil in the Empire. The emperor in power was Diocletian. He came to power eight years before I was born. Like many emperors before him, he was having a difficult time governing such a vast empire. One of the problems was that to protect such a large border against the barbarians, he needed a strong army. However, a strong army was a threat to his power. This is a great lesson from history. Julius Caesar gained his power mostly from the allegiance the military had for him. So Diocletian divided the army into smaller, more manageable units to keep them from being a threat to him the way one strong military leader like Caesar or Diocletian himself had been.

Another problem he had was that there was too much bureaucracy for him to manage by himself. So he split the empire in half with Diocletian ruling the eastern half and Maximian ruling the west. Diocletian was of Greek heritage and was probably more comfortable in the east. He very rarely visited Rome. Under Maximian and himself there were two heirs-apparent to the empire. Thus, these four men were called the Tetrarchs, the four rulers.

Since there was too much bureaucracy and too little of the known world left to conquer, Diocletian had nowhere to go to collect new funds from treasuries of conquered peoples. So he made every free man in the empire a Roman citizen to increase the tax base. He also increased the taxes on everyone else as well.

He also decided that Christianity had to go. One might wonder why. We were good Roman citizens. We paid our taxes. We fed the poor and needy. We didn't commit crimes or murder. The problem was that we didn't worship their gods. Not only that, but we did not even acknowledge their existence. With everything that was going badly with the empire and as superstitious as they were, they probably thought it was our fault that things were politically and economically falling apart. As I have mentioned before, the Romans were very religious. Diocletian felt very threatened by Christians who would not worship him as a god. He didn't trust anyone who wasn't totally subservient to the state. There needed to be a revival of Roman religion.

In February of A.D. 303, Diocletian published an edict that would change all of our lives. All copies of our scripture had to be surrendered and burned. All of the churches were to be destroyed. We were not allowed to hold Christian meetings. All of our civil rights were taken away. My father could no longer hold public office. We were now subject to torture after trial no matter our social status. Christians who were slaves could not be freed.

The news of this edict finally reached Rome during Holy Week of that year. We were all outraged. My mother and I were on our way to the church to help prepare for the celebration of the Last Supper, and we could see the smoke from a fire. It was the church burning. I couldn't believe my eyes. Almost all of the copies of scripture the church had were in there. I really couldn't understand why we were hated so badly. Mother and I just kept walking. It was no use to try to put out the fire.

When we arrived at home, Mother told Father, "It has started again. They've burned the church. What are we going to do?"

Father replied, "We must meet with Father Lucius and the other church elders. Agnes, help your mother bake the bread for communion this evening."

There was a knock at the door. We froze in fear. We were active in the church. Many people were witnesses to our faith. I saw some of the books of scripture I had been reading laying out on a table. I calmly walked over and gathered them up as one of our servants went to answer the door. I hid the books in my room. I prayed. I couldn't hear who was at the door or what was happening. Fear overwhelmed me.

"Lord God, please protect us from evil. Lord, watch over us. Help us to remain strong in our faith. We know You are coming soon. Please be with us. Keep me from fear. Calm my heart. Grant me peace." His warmth blanketed me as I prayed. He took my fear away. I realized at that moment what I needed to do.

The last thing Jesus needed was for His children to cower in fear before the hands of the enemy. I knew I must continue to live as Christ would want. I had no other desire than to be completely devoted to Him. Someone must stand up against this evil. I must do my part.

"Agnes!" My mother was calling to me.

"Yes, Mother," I replied. I had no idea how long she had been looking for me.

"I need your help with the bread."

"Who was at the door?"

"It was Father Lucius."

"Thank God." I slumped on my bed in relief.

"We are going to meet this evening in the catacombs. What is the matter?" She must have seen the marks of tears on my face.

"I was so afraid that they would arrest us and take us away. I was afraid they would take our books."

"You look more angry than afraid, child."

"That's because I am, and I'm pretty sure God is too."

"You are probably right, but this baking won't wait much longer."

"Mother?"

"Yes, dear."

"I've decided not to get married. I want to give myself completely to Jesus."

"Are you sure? This decision could cause lots of problems."

"It doesn't much matter now. Does it? I mean what I am is illegal anyway. I will not deny my Lord. These evil men are going to try to take everything from us. I cannot let them take away who I am."

"I understand what you are saying. Oh, my dear child." Mother took me in her arms and held me close. "Let's go make some bread."

We got the bread ready, and the whole family went to the catacombs to celebrate the Last Supper of Christ. We climbed down the steps to where our persecuted forefathers are buried and where they worshiped in secret.

We had to carry torches quite a way down the corridors because it was pitch black. Then, off in the distance, I could see a light. We extinguished our torches as we approached the chapel. Oh, what a sight! Some of the other members of our community had lit small oil lamps and set them all about the chamber. It was so beautiful to see the light bouncing off the beautiful frescoes on the walls.

We all gathered around and sang a hymn to the Lord. We sang of His life and His sacrifice. We sang of the bread and wine and how we are the body of Christ. In my heart I wished that we could defy the authorities and continue to worship in public.

It came time in the service for confession and repentance. I wondered if I was sinning by not wanting to obey the law of Rome. Would my decision not to marry upset my father? Would it be a sin to go against his wishes if he wants me to marry? I really needed to talk to him.

"Lord, have mercy. Christ, have mercy. Lord, have mercy."

"The first reading is from the book of Exodus:

'In the morning there was a layer of dew around the camp. When the dew was gone, the ground was covered with a thin layer of flakes like frost on the ground. When the Israelites saw it, they asked each other, "What is this?"

because they didn't know what it was.

Moses said to them, "It's the food the Lord has given you to eat. This is what the Lord has commanded: Each of you should gather as much as you can eat. Take two quarts for each person in your tent."

So that is what the Israelites did. Some gathered more, some less. They measured it into two-quart containers. Those who had gathered more didn't have too much. Those who had gathered less didn't have too little. They gathered as much as they could eat.

Then Moses said to them, "No one may keep any of it until morning."

But some of them didn't listen to Moses. They kept part of it until morning, and it was full of worms and smelled bad. So Moses was angry with them.

Each morning they gathered as much food as they could eat. When the sun was hot, it melted away. But on the sixth day they gathered twice as much food, for quarts per person. All the leaders of the community came to Moses and told him about it.

He said to them, "This is what the Lord said: Tomorrow is a day of worship, a holy day of worship dedicated to the Lord. Bake what you want to bake, and boil what you want to boil. Save all that's left over, and keep it until tomorrow morning."

So they saved it until the next morning as Moses had commanded, but it didn't smell or have worms in it. "Eat it today," Moses said, "because today is a day of worship dedicated to the Lord. You won't find anything on the ground today. You can gather food on six days, but on the seventh day, the day of worship, you won't find any."

On the seventh day some people went out to gather food, but they didn't find any. The Lord said to Moses, "How long will you refuse to do what I have commanded and instructed you to do? Remember: The Lord has given you this day of worship. That's why he gives you enough food on the sixth day for two days. On the seventh day you may not leave. Everyone, stay where you are." So the people never worked on the seventh day of the week.

The Israelites called the food *manna*. It was like coriander seeds. It was white and tasted like wafers made with honey.'

"This is the word of the Lord."

"Thanks be to God," we responded.

Next we recited a responsorial psalm. Father Lucius led us, "The Lord is my shepherd. I am never in need."

We responded, "He makes me lie down in green pastures. He leads me beside peaceful waters."

"He renews my soul. He guides me along the paths of righteousness for the sake of his name."

"Even though I walk through the dark valley of death, because you are with me, I fear no harm. Your rod and your staff give me courage."

"You prepare a banquet for me while my enemies watch. You anoint my head with oil. My cup overflows."

"Certainly, goodness and mercy will stay close to me all the days of my life, and I will remain in the Lord's house for days without end," we concluded.

"The second reading is from the Letter of Paul to the Romans: 'Now the way to receive God's approval has been made plain in a way other than Moses' Teachings. Moses' Teachings and the Prophets tell us this. Everyone who believes has God's approval through faith in Jesus Christ.

There is no difference between people. Because all people have sinned, they have fallen short of God's glory. They receive God's approval freely by an act of his kindness through the price Christ Jesus paid to set us free from sin. God showed that Christ is the throne of mercy where God's approval is given through faith in Christ's blood. In his patience God waited to deal with sins committed in the past. He waited so that he could display his approval at the present time. This shows that he is a God of justice, a God who approves of people who believe in Jesus.

So, do we have anything to brag about? Bragging has been eliminated. On what basis was it eliminated? On the basis of our own efforts? No, indeed! Rather, it is eliminated on the basis of faith. We conclude that a person has God's approval because of faith, not because of his own efforts.'

"This is the word of the Lord."

"Thanks be to God."

"Please rise for the reading from the Gospel of Mark:

'While they were at the table eating, Jesus said, "I can guarantee this truth: One of you is going to betray me, one who is eating with me!"

Feeling hurt, they asked him one by one, "You don't mean me, do you?"

He said to them, "It's one of you twelve, someone dipping his hand into the bowl with me. The Son of Man is going to die as the Scriptures say he will. But how horrible it will be for that person who betrays the Son of Man! It would have been better for that person if he had never been born."

While they were eating, Jesus took bread and blessed it. He broke the bread, gave it to them, and said, "Take this. This is my body."

Then he took a cup, spoke a prayer of thanksgiving, and gave the cup to them. They all drank from it. He said to them, "This is my blood, the blood of the promise. It is poured out for many people.

"I can guarantee this truth: I won't drink this wine again until that day when I drink new wine in the kingdom of God."

After they sang a hymn, they went to the Mount of Olives. Then Jesus said to them, "All of you will abandon me. Scripture says, 'I will strike the shepherd, and the sheep will be scattered.'

"But after I am brought back to life, I will go to Galilee ahead of you."

Peter said to him, "Even if everyone else abandons you, I won't."

Jesus said to Peter, "I can guarantee this truth: Tonight, before a rooster crows twice, you will say three times that you don't know me."

But Peter said very strongly, "Even if I have to die with you, I will never say that I don't know you." All the other disciples said the same thing.

Then they came to a place called Gethsemane. He said to his disciples, "Stay here while I pray."

He took Peter, James, and John with him and began to feel distressed and anguished. He said to them, "My anguish is so great that I feel as if I'm dying. Wait here, and stay awake."

After walking a little farther, he fell to the ground and prayed that if it were possible he might not have to suffer what was ahead of him. He said, "Abba! Father! You can do anything. Take this cup of suffering away from me. But let your will be done rather than mine."

He went back and found them asleep. He said to Peter, "Simon, are you sleeping? Couldn't you stay awake for one hour? Stay awake, and pray that you won't be tempted. You want to do what's right, but you're weak."

He went away again and prayed the same prayer as before. He found them asleep because they couldn't keep their eyes open. They didn't even know what they should say to him. He came back a third time and said to them, "You might as well sleep now. It's all over. The time has come for the Son of Man to be handed over to sinners. Get up! Let's go! The one who is betraying me is near."

Just then, while Jesus was still speaking, Judas, one of the twelve apostles, arrived. A crowd carrying swords and clubs was with him. They were from the chief priests, scribes, and leaders of the people. Now, the traitor had given them a signal. He said, "The one I kiss is the man you want. Arrest him, and guard him closely as you take him away."

Then Judas quickly stepped up to Jesus and said, "Rabbi!" and kissed him.

Some men took hold of Jesus and arrested him. One of those standing there pulled out his sword and cut off the ear of the chief priest's servant.

Jesus asked them, "Have you come out with swords and clubs to arrest me as if I were a criminal? I used to teach in the temple courtyard every day. But you didn't arrest me then. But what the Scriptures say must come true."

Then all the disciples abandoned him and ran away.

A certain young man was following Jesus. He had nothing on but a linen sheet. They tried to arrest him, but he left the linen sheet behind and ran away naked.'

"This is the gospel of the Lord."

"Praise be to you, Lord Jesus Christ."

"Please sit down everyone," Father Lucius began to address us. "We are entering some difficult times. Some of us who are old enough can remember previous times like these. Jesus even told us that we would have hardships. Look at Paul and what he suffered.

"We must remember that the time we have here is fleeting. We must focus on eternity, especially now. We don't know if He is coming back tomorrow or next year, but He is coming back. We must be ready for Him.

"We cannot waiver in our faith. It will be very tempting. You will be tempted to lie about your faith. You will be tempted to bow down to their idols and offer sacrifices. You will be tempted to publicly deny Christ to save your life.

"Government officials will threaten to kill you. You may be afraid for your life or that of your family. I understand. God understands. However, we must be brave. We must remember that we already have eternal life. This life was bought and paid for by Jesus Christ. We have nothing to fear. What can the world give us that Christ has not? We are a part of His kingdom. He promised us that He will come back for us, and we <u>must</u> be ready. If we are sacrificing and praying to the gods of Rome, even just for show, we will not be ready.

"Remember the sacrifice of Jesus Christ. Remember His promise to us. Do not forget about what he has done for us. He loves us. He wants us to love him back. He wants us to show the love we share with him to the world. We must love those who will persecute us. When we do this, we are being whom Christ wants us to be."

At this point all those who were not baptized were asked to leave. We then recited the Apostles' Creed, "I believe in God, the Father almighty, creator of heaven and earth; and in Jesus Christ, His only Son, our Lord; who was conceived by the Holy Spirit, born of the Virgin Mary, suffered under Pontius Pilate, was crucified, died, and was buried. He descended into hell; the third day he arose again from the dead; he ascended into heaven, sits at the right hand of God, the Father almighty; whence He shall come to judge the living and the dead. I believe in the Holy Spirit, the holy Catholic Church, the communion of saints, the forgiveness of sins, the resurrection of the body, and life everlasting. Amen."

Next we sang a hymn as the offering was collected and the elements for Holy Communion were brought to the altar.

Father Lucius prayed as he took the bread that Mother and I made into his hands, "Blessed are you, Lord, God of all creation. Through your goodness we have this bread to offer, which earth has given and human hands have made. It will become for us the bread of life."

We replied, "Blessed be God forever."

Next he took the wine and prayed, "Blessed are you, Lord, God of all creation. Through your goodness we have this wine to offer, fruit of the vine and work of human hands. It will become our spiritual drink."

Again we responded, "Blessed be God forever."

Father Lucius then said, "Pray that our sacrifice may be acceptable to God, the almighty Father."

"May the Lord accept the sacrifice at your hands for the praise and glory of his name, for our good, and the good of all his Church," we answered.

Father Lucius then said, "The Lord be with you."

"And also with you."

"Lift up your hearts."

"We lift them up to the Lord."

"Let us give thanks to the Lord our God."

"It is right to give Him thanks and praise."

"We come to you, Father, with praise and thanksgiving, through Jesus Christ, your son. Through Him we ask you to accept and bless these gifts we offer you in sacrifice.

"We offer them for your holy church, watch over it, Lord, and guide it; grant it peace and unity throughout the world. We offer them for all who hold and teach the faith that comes to us from the apostles. Remember, Lord, your people, especially those for whom we now pray."

There was a moment of silence as we prayed. I prayed for my parents because I knew the hardship they may suffer from the decision that I made.

"Remember all of us gathered here before you. You know how firmly we believe in you and dedicate ourselves to you. We offer you this sacrifice of praise for ourselves and those who are dear to us. We pray to you, our living and true God, for our well being and redemption.

"In union with the whole Church we honor Mary, the mother of Jesus Christ our Lord and God. We honor Joseph, her husband, the apostles and martyrs Peter, and Paul, Andrew, and all the saints. May their merits and prayers gain us your constant help and protection. Father, accept this offering from your whole family. Grant us your peace in this life, save us from final damnation, and count us among those you have chosen.

"Bless and approve our offering; make it acceptable to you, an offering in spirit and in truth. Let it become for us the body and blood of Jesus Christ, your only son, our Lord.

"The day before he suffered he took bread in his sacred hands and looking up to heaven, to you, his almighty Father, he gave you thanks and praise. He broke the bread, gave it to his disciples and said: Take this, all of you, and eat it: this is my body, which will be given up for you." Father Lucius raised the bread toward heaven and then placed it back onto the altar.

"When supper was ended, he took the cup. Again he gave you thanks and praise, gave the cup to his disciples, and said: Take this, all of you, and drink from it: this is the cup of my blood, the blood of the new and everlasting covenant. It will be shed for you and for all so that sins may be forgiven. Do this in memory of me." Father Lucius raised the cup toward heaven and then returned it to the altar.

He then said, "Let us proclaim the mystery of faith."

We replied, "When we eat this bread and drink this cup, we proclaim your death, Lord Jesus, until you come in glory."

Father Lucius continued, "Father, we celebrate the memory of Christ, your Son. We, your people and your ministers, recall his passion, his resurrection from the dead, and his ascension into glory; and from the many gifts you have given us we offer to you, God of glory and majesty, this holy and perfect sacrifice: the bread of life and the cup of eternal salvation. Look with favor on these offerings and accept them as once you accepted the gifts of your servant Abel, the sacrifice of Abraham, our father in faith, and the bread and wine offered by your priest Melchisedech. Almighty God, we pray that your angel may take this sacrifice to your altar in heaven. Then, as we receive from this altar the sacred body and blood of your Son, let us be filled with every grace and blessing.

"Remember, Lord, those who have died and have gone before us marked with the sign of faith, especially those for whom we now pray."

Again we prayed in silence.

" May these, and all who sleep in Christ, find in your presence light, happiness, and peace.

"For ourselves, too, we ask some share in the fellowship of your apostles and martyrs, with John the Baptist, Stephen, Matthias, Barnabas, and all the saints. Though we are sinners, we trust in your mercy and love. Do not consider what we truly deserve, but grant us your forgiveness.

"Through Christ our Lord you give us all these gifts. You fill them with life and goodness; you bless them and make them holy.

"Through him, with him, in him, in the unity of the Holy Spirit, all glory and honor is yours, almighty Father, forever and ever."

"Amen," we cried.

"Let us pray with confidence to the Father in the words our Savior gave us."

"Our Father, who is in heaven, holy be your name; your kingdom come; your will be done on earth as it is in heaven. Give us this day our daily bread; and forgive us our trespasses as we forgive those who trespass against us; and lead us not into temptation, but deliver us from evil."

Father Lucius continued, "Deliver us, Lord, from every evil, and grant us peace in our day. In your mercy keep us free from sin and protect us from all anxiety as we wait in joyful hope for the coming of our Savior, Jesus Christ."

"For the kingdom, the power, and the glory are yours, now and forever," we responded.

"The peace of the Lord be with you always."

"And also with you."

"Let us offer each other the sign of peace." At this point we gave each other hugs and kisses to show each other the love of Christ that is in us.

Father Lucius then took the body of Christ into his hands. He said, "Lamb of God, you take away the sins of the world: have mercy on us. Lamb of God, you take away the sins of the world: have mercy on us. Lamb of God, you take away the sins of the world: grant us peace."

He then said, "This is the Lamb of God who takes away the sins of the world. Happy are those who are called to his supper."

We replied, "Lord, I am not worthy to receive you, but only say the word and I shall be healed."

Father Lucius then ate a piece of the body of Christ. Then he drank a sip of the blood of Christ. After this we each had an opportunity to eat and drink the body of Christ. When it was my turn, I took the body and held it in my hand and remembered what he did for me by dying. As I took Jesus' body into my mouth I could feel his love for me. As I drank his blood, it tasted sweet. I truly felt in communion with him.

Once we had all received the sacrament Father Lucius said, "The Lord be with you."

"And also with you."

"May almighty God bless you, the Father, the Son, and the Holy Spirit."

"Amen."

Father Lucius asked the group if there were any announcements to be made. There weren't any. It was decided that this would be our meeting place until we were forced to move by the authorities. Lucius then said, "May the blessing of almighty God, the Father, and the Son, and the Holy Spirit, come upon you and remain with you forever."

"Amen."

"Go in peace to love and serve the Lord."

"Thanks be to God."

We sang one last hymn and then went back up to the street. My mind was made up, and I needed to tell my father what I had chosen to do. I must admit that I was filled with apprehension because I didn't know how he would react. All in all he was a good Roman and ran his house as a Roman would. If he said that I couldn't consecrate my life to Christ, then I wouldn't.

## 3

The sermon that Lucius gave galvanized me. Being that I am a woman, I really didn't have anything to lose. If I were to marry, it would be for the betterment of the man that married me because I would be a good match for someone. My dowry would be large because of my father's social status. I really needed to think and pray on how I would approach my father. I spent the rest of the night coming up with answers to his questions.

The next morning I spoke to my mother about it again. She was afraid for me, but she could understand why I wanted to do this. She told me that Father would be home after the midday meal and that I could talk to him then. Since my father was an astute businessman, I knew I had to have very good reasons for what I wanted to do. I prayed for wisdom and guidance from God. He would give me the words I needed when the time came.

After we had finished eating, the servants cleared away the rest of the food and the dirty dishes. About an hour later my father arrived at home. I had gone to my room, not having eaten much because of nerves. He knocked on my door. "Hello," he said.

I stood up out of respect. "Hello, Father," I replied.

"Your mother tells me that you have something to tell me."

"Yes. I wanted to ask your permission to choose the man I will serve for the rest of my life."

"You are so young. Has a young man already swept you off your feet?"

"I wouldn't say that he is a young man, but yes, my heart has been claimed."

"Do I know him?"

"I would hope so."

"Who is he?"

"I have decided to give my life completely to Jesus Christ."

My father sat down with a thoughtful look on his face. "You already did that when you were confirmed into the faith last year."

"No, Father. I mean I want to consecrate my life to Him."

My father's expression became more concerned. "You do know what this means, especially since the Emperor has issued this edict banning Christianity."

"Yes, I do."

"Do you? It's hard enough being a Christian as it is. You are old enough now to wed. Suitors are going to begin calling on you very soon."

"Yes, Mother has already informed me of what is expected of me. Frankly, I don't want to do what Rome expects of me. I want to live a pure life close to Christ. I want to stand up against this evil.

"Christ has already won my hand as well as my heart. I understand if you must disown me to protect yourself and the family. I don't believe that I have anything to lose.

"If I wed an earthly husband, I will be giving up my identity. I will be doing my womanly duty to Rome to bear her more pagan children. I cannot do it. I cannot turn my back on Jesus especially in these terrible times."

"You will lose more than your identity if you pursue this course. You will probably lose your life," my father replied sternly.

"I have already thought about that. Didn't Jesus lose his life for me? What a wonderful way to show the world our love for Jesus than to lay down our lives for Him! Look at Peter and Paul, Father."

"Yes, but they were old men who had lived their lives."

"They were old men who had lived their lives dedicated to Jesus. They lost everything the world holds dear for Him.

"Father, I am a woman. In the eyes of Rome, I am only worth how many children I can give her and how many riches I can bring to my husband. In the eyes of Christ, I am much more than that. I am a beloved child of God who is free to choose how to live my life in His will. Do you want me to be bound to this evil society? I want to remain pure for my Lord."

"I see you have made up your mind. I will speak to your mother about this." He got up and left me alone with my thoughts.

That morning I had been studying with Hector while my father was gone conducting business. We were reading the *Aeneid* by Virgil. It was interesting, but it was hard for me to stay focused. What would Father say about my decision? What would happen to me as a result? Would I be found out? Would I be killed?

Jesus was killed for his beliefs. The Jews were afraid of Rome. Rome. Romans would like to think they are the pinnacle of civilization, but they are amoral and worldly. Human life is insignificant to them. All that is important is the State. Jesus didn't teach that.

Jesus taught that all people are important, not just rich men. Women, children, slaves, and the diseased have the same right to salvation as any man. I felt pretty special since I fall into two of those categories. He died for me. He died, so I could be with Him in heaven.

The next day found me studying in the garden. It was a lovely spring morning. The breeze caressed my hair and face, and the sun shone brightly. I could see my father approaching to sit down next to me out of the corner of my eye. He had a very serious look on his face.

"What are you reading?" he asked.

"Virgil," I replied. He wasn't here to discuss my studies, but it wasn't my place to force the issue. I might have been a headstrong, willful, young lady, but I knew where I stood with my father's authority.

"Your mother and I have been discussing what you have decided to do with your life. We are joyful and sad at the same time. We are extremely happy that you have such devotion to our Lord and are proud that you have decided to stand up for what is good and just.

"On the other hand, we also know, as you do, the grave consequences that could befall you if you choose this course for your life. You are a beautiful, intelligent, young woman who will be expected to marry soon. You would make a fine wife for any young suitor."

"Father, I have prayed long and hard about this. I am at peace. Whatever happens to me, God will use me for His greater glory."

"You are much braver than I am, my lamb. Your mother and I have decided that you may follow Christ however he is calling you, but we will not be able to stand by you when you go before the Church.

"I hope that you understand that I must protect my livelihood. I know that I must trust God, but I also have my household to support. I believe that God will understand that I am giving my daughter to him. If anything happens to you, your mother and I will not be able to save you."

"Oh, Father! I have already been saved. I don't expect you to give up your life for me. Jesus has already done that."

"I look at you and see a small child; but you open your mouth, and I hear a wise young woman. May God protect us and grant us peace." He took me into his arms and held me close. Tears ran down both of our cheeks.

God had answered my prayers. I knew that my parents would not be able to fully stand by me even though I had hoped they would. I knew now what I would do at church tomorrow on Resurrection Sunday.

Morning dawned brightly. The sun shone beautifully through the graceful pine trees. My family and I went to the catacombs in secret to celebrate our risen Lord. It was ironic that we were going to a tomb to celebrate the Resurrection much in the same way that Mary went to the tomb the day Christ rose from the dead.

What a wonderful experience that must have been! Going to a place where you knew there was a body that had been dead for three days, only to be told by an angel that the body you were looking for wasn't there. The angel told Mary that Jesus is risen. I probably would have been frightened just like Mary was.

Despite the edict from Diocletian, there were many people in attendance for worship. The chapel was well lit with oil lamps. It was beautiful. The story of Christ's rising from the dead was read. Father Lucius spoke again on how this new persecution is like Christ's suffering on the cross. He told about how those who die for their faith will receive glory in heaven, and the Church will grow stronger from their example.

As I listened to the sermon, I wondered about what I was doing. Was my goal to be a martyr for the faith? I didn't think it was. I wanted to show my love for Christ through purity. I loved life and didn't wish for death. My God is the God of life. The world is a world of death. It is our duty to bring life to the world.

During communion I was in constant prayer: in prayer for my family, the church, and our enemies. I wished that they could only know what joy could be had in being free from the shackles of worldly lust and earthly desires. I also prayed that God would be with me as I announced my consecration to the congregation.

As I partook of the Body of Christ, I truly felt his presence with me. I could feel his love for me. I praised God in my heart that He could love me so much that he would allow his Son to die just for me. I believed that I was making the right decision about my life.

When communion was finished, Father Lucius went up to the front of the chapel and asked if anyone had any announcements to make to the church community. My heart leaped into my throat. This was it. I rose from my seat and went to stand next to Father Lucius. "What do you have to say, Agnes?"

I tried desperately to keep my voice from shaking. "I want to let this gathering know that from this day forward I am consecrating myself to Jesus Christ. I consider Him to be my husband. I want to give all I am to His service."

The priest was a little taken aback by my words. He paused briefly to consider his response. "The church is happy to receive your commitment to the risen Lord. We promise to stand with you as you make your journey with Him. May you be like Christ's bride, the Church, and may you continue to be pure in heart, mind, and spirit.

"May God bless you, Agnes, in the name of the Father, of the Son, and of the Holy Spirit."

"Amen," I replied.

"And may his blessing fall upon the whole church and remain with you forever, in the name of the Father, of the Son, and of the Holy Spirit."

"Amen," the congregation replied.

"Go in peace to love and serve our Lord."

"Thanks be to God."

# 4

The next few weeks were mostly uneventful. We continued to worship in the catacombs. I began going to the marketplace and help with purchasing necessities for our home, and I continued with my studies. My monthly flow also started. I was now of the age to marry.

One beautiful day I went down to the market at the Campus Marcius. The sun was shining, and the blue sky was reflected in the Tiber River. God has truly blessed humanity with His gift of nature. I had stopped to pick out some fruit from a vendor when a handsome young man came and stood next to me.

He said, "This one looks good." He handed me an apple that had a nasty bruise on one side.

I laughed as I took it to examine it more closely. I said, "It might be good for feeding swine. No offense."

"None taken. How about this one?" He handed me a beautiful, ripe apple.

"This one is perfect. Thank you."

"What is your name?"

"Agnes Clodia. What's yours?"

"Marcus Herculeus, son of Prefect Maximum Herculeus."

"He sounds important."

"He is, and you're beautiful." My heart leaped into my throat. No man had ever spoken to me that way before. I said a silent prayer to keep myself calm. "You are blushing. I am sorry if I embarrassed you."

"I'm sorry. I am only accustomed to speaking to my father, my brothers, and my tutor. I really don't know how to respond." That was the truth. I really didn't. I wanted to run away and lock myself in my room and never re-emerge. That way I could not be tempted to abandon Christ for a handsome man.

"Don't be afraid. I probably was a bit forward. Would you mind if I went to your home and called on you formally?"

Then I really began to panic. His father was a prefect. If I refused, my family could get into trouble. If I accepted, he might get the wrong idea and think that I was interested in courtship. Then, I thought that meeting him at my home would be a wonderful opportunity to feel him out about talking to him about Jesus. I had opened my mouth about giving my life to God. It was time for me to show Him that I meant what I said.

"You may call on me. When can I expect your visit, so I may be ready for you?"

"I will come see you the day after tomorrow, on Saturn's day."

"Wonderful. I will see you then." I was so excited I could hardly contain myself. I couldn't wait to tell my parents. This was the first opportunity I had ever really had to talk to a non-believer about Jesus.

I finally paid for my apples. I'm sure the vendor thought we would make a good match by the way she was smiling knowingly at me. If she only knew what my plans were, she probably would not understand.

Saturn's day arrived, and I could not keep still. I had spoken to my mother about what was expected of me when a man came to call. I also explained to her why I had accepted his advances despite my promise to Jesus. I had to keep up appearances to protect my family, if not myself. There was a knock on the outer door to the villa. A servant came in to let me know that there was a young gentleman by the name of Marcus Tillius Herculeus calling.

*This is it*, I thought to myself. "You may show him in."

A few moments later, there he was. He was stunningly handsome in a beautiful white toga with embroidery around the edges. I took more notice of him now than I had the other day in the market, but he had a strong, handsome face with beautiful brown eyes and what looked like soft brown hair. *Lead me not into temptation*, I prayed.

"Hello, Marcus Tillius Herculeus." I said it laughingly because I was not used to such formality.

"Hello, Agnes Clodia Cresentiana." He laughed as well. He was very friendly.

"May I ask your permission to escort you to the Forum. The festival of Vesta is being celebrated."

This was a very important festival for Rome. Vesta was the goddess of the hearth. There was an eternal flame that symbolized the hearth of Rome in her temple. The Vestal virgins, the tenders of the temple and flame, were not allowed to marry. How like them I was! But I could not let Marcus know that, not now.

"I would be delighted. Let's go."

We left my home and went down to the Forum. The temples were beautiful and there were streamers everywhere. The walkways were covered in flowers. Only foot traffic was allowed on the Forum, except the Vestal virgins were allowed to ride in chariots so they would not have to tread on the ground.

Marcus and I began to get to know each other. He had been given a good education as I had, so we had much to talk about. We debated Plato and the wisdom of Socrates. I avoided religious subjects on purpose. He never brought them up. I really liked this young man. Would I ever be able to tell him the whole truth about me?

Several months passed. Marcus came to call on me frequently. I attended but did not participate in the sacrifice to Hercules in August. Marcus' family is rumored to have been descendant from him, so it was important to him. I really enjoyed his company, and I was beginning to have feelings for him.

Then, one afternoon in November when he came to call, he told me that he had told his father, Maximum, about me. This was very dangerous for me because that meant that Marcus was considering me as a potential bride. I was also secretly happy because I had won his heart. Hopefully, he could trust me, and I could now begin to talk to him about Jesus.

"My father is pleased with you," he told me. "You will be a good match for me, he thinks. You are smart and beautiful. It doesn't hurt that you will have a good dowry."

"I am flattered. I am going to need to discuss this with my family."

"May I speak with your father?"

"Let me talk to him first."

"I love you."

He loves me. *Oh, Lord, what am I supposed to do now?* A calming peace came over me. The Holy Spirit was with me. "I love you, too, Marcus."

He took me into his arms and embraced me. This was not the embrace that was exchanged at worship. This was something more powerful. My head knew that I needed to pull away, but my heart didn't want to. It was confusing. I desperately needed to talk to my mother and father.

When he released me, he looked into my eyes which I averted. He asked, "What is wrong?"

I replied, "I am so happy and nervous. I didn't realize this could happen so fast."

"I understand. I am excited also."

With that he turned and left. My heart was beating so hard that it felt as if it was going to leap out of my chest. I ran off to the back of the house to speak with my mother.

The next time Marcus came to call he spoke with my father. I had already spoken to him about what Marcus was planning to do. I told him not to tell him about my commitment to Christ. That would be my responsibility. If there were to be any repercussions, they would be mine to bear.

After Marcus spoke with my father he came running up to me.

"He said, 'Yes.'!"

A lump rose in my throat. "Good. I am glad." I left it at that. Soon I would start witnessing to him about Jesus.

The next day we went to the Colosseum to watch the Plebian games. At least he wanted to watch the games. I did not want to go. The games were barbaric. God did not like the waste of human life that the games caused. While we were walking, I asked him, "Do you really enjoy the games?"

"Yes, they are thrilling. I really enjoy watching the skilled gladiators. They fight to honor the gods."

Here was my moment. "Do you really believe in all those gods?"

"I don't know. Why?"

"They seem too human to me with all of their rivalry and jealousy. I don't know that I trust a god like Jupiter who follows the whims of his lust."

"I hadn't really thought about it that way."

"I prefer a God that is all powerful and not at the mercy of 'human' desires."

He stopped in his tracks. A thrill of fear rose in my chest. "Is there something wrong?" I asked. He grabbed my arm and pulled me over to an alley.

When he had taken me several feet into the alley, he said, "'A god' - that's what you said? 'A god!' You sound like one of those Christian cultists."

"So what if I do?"

"So what if you do?" He began to pace.

"What's the matter?"

"I think you do." He then grabbed both of my arms and pressed me up against the wall. "Do you know what happens to Christians?"

"Yes. We are arrested, tried in puppet courts for treason, and offered up as human sacrifices in the theater to your 'gods.'"

"So you are a Christian."

"Yes."

Marcus just stared at me. I didn't know what to say to him, so I waited. He let go of my arms and turned his back to me. "What do you want from me?" he asked. "I hold your very life in my hands. Do you know what would happen if I told my father about this?"

"He would have me arrested. I would be killed."

"You are right."

"You don't have to tell him though."

"Don't you people teach that you should not lie?"

"Yes, but what if he doesn't ask?"

"What would we do if we were to marry?"

I was silent at that. Marriage would break the vow I took before the church. "I have a confession."

"What now?"

"I haven't been completely honest with you. I wanted to get close to you because you are potentially a powerful person. I wanted to show you that Christians aren't really a threat to Rome. We love Rome. We just don't love her gods."

"How haven't you been honest with me?"

"I have given my life completely to God. I am married to Him already."

"So where do I fit into this picture?"

"I care about you. You are a good person. I wanted to share the love of Jesus with you."

"Why should Jesus care about me?"

"He loves you. He died for you, so you would have a place with him in Paradise."

"Is Elisium not enough?"

"Our ideas of heaven are similar. The Christian version has God there loving each and every one of us the same."

"Let's go."

"Where are we going?"

"Away from here. I don't want you to have to watch what is going on at the Coliseum."

"Why not?"

"They are killing Christians there today."

I was silent. I knew what was at stake. Marcus did hold my life in his hands. Yet I believed that I could trust him completely. The only question was what his father might do. What would Marcus do? He had already asked my father for my hand. My father had given his blessing. Now, I was refusing him. I had no idea what he was thinking. We weren't safe speaking in public, but I had an idea. "We need to go somewhere that we can talk."

I took his hand and led him to a secret entrance to the catacombs. I lit a torch, and we went down to one of our places of worship. "Why are you bringing me here?" he asked. "This will bring danger on you and your family."

"I want to tell you why I would follow a God who is forbidden," I whispered in his ear. It was a marvelous secret that the Roman government wanted to keep from him.

"I would like to know. It doesn't make sense."

"God loves you. God loves me. He loves all of humanity."

"What love are you talking about?"

"The Greeks have a word for it - *agape*. Unconditional, never ending love. He loved us so much that He sacrificed his son to save us from sin."

"Sin?"

"The wages of sin is death. We believe that we should live a good life. Love God and love each other."

"What is sin?"

"Doing wrong. Murder. Adultery. Theft. Covetousness. Lying. Dishonor of your parents. Not worshiping the one True God."

"Why are you telling me this?"

"I love you. I want you to know the Truth."

"Marry me."

"I cannot. You know my commitment to Christ."

"Why?"

"To show Rome that her way is wrong."

"You are insane."

"Maybe. Rome is not failing because of Christians. She is failing because of her insatiable thirst for world domination."

"You are speaking treason. You are too trusting. What do I tell my father? I've already told him that your father agreed to our marriage."

"You will do what you need to do. Don't worry about me. God is with me. He has a plan for my life."

"I will tell my father the truth. You are in love with another suitor. I promise that I will never tell him about this place."

"Thank you. I hope I will see you again."

"That I cannot promise."

I brought him back to the surface. We said our goodbyes and went our separate ways. I knew that events that were to shape the rest of my life were now in motion.

# 5

The next day there was a knock on our front door. It was Marcus and his father Maximum. One of our servants answered the door and announced that Maximum wished to speak to my father. My father invited him into our dining room to talk.

They were talking about me, but I was not allowed to listen in on the conversation. Mother and I went out into the garden. I sat on a bench and prayed. About a half an hour later my father came out of the house and sat next to me. He let out a long sigh before he began to speak. "Now you have done it. Maximum says that you are no longer interested in marrying Marcus."

"You knew that I never intended to marry him." I stared straight ahead. Fear of anger from my father rose in my chest like a flame.

"Agnes, look at me." I hesitated. Then, I turned my head and looked him squarely in the eye. He placed his hands on my shoulders. "Your life is in danger. You have been playing with fire."

I paused again before I spoke. I was still a child in his eyes. "Do you think that I don't know about the danger I have placed myself in? What I am doing I am doing for the future of the Church. As a community we will not survive until someone stands up to Rome."

"I don't want to lose you. I love you, lamb." He wrapped me in his strong arms and held me tight.

"I know that, Daddy, but I believe that this is what God wants me to do." Tears welled up in both of our eyes. I sobbed, "I'm sorry."

"Why has He called upon you?"

"I am a virgin. They cannot by their own laws put me to death. How will they justify it?"

"Oh, I am sure they will find a way."

"Have you ever thought why they are so afraid of us?"

"We do not worship Rome. They truly believe that we are turning their gods against them."

"So what is Maximum going to do?"

"He gave me a little time to talk some sense into you."

"I guess you are not talking much sense into me. Are you?"

"I knew I wouldn't be able to convince you. He says that if you will change your mind and marry Marcus, he will not condemn you as a Christian publicly."

"What about the rest of the family?"

"He says that he will leave us out of it. I will tell him that you are misguided and have made this decision all on your own."

A shudder of relief passed over my body. "At least that part of my prayers has been answered."

"There is another condition."

"What?"

"You must offer a sacrifice to the goddess Minerva."

"No. I will never break the Commandments and do that."

"I know." He was silent.

Another long pause fell upon our conversation. I finally asked, "How much time do you have to talk 'sense' into me?"

"He gave me a month. You have until the beginning of January to decide to marry Marcus or to produce the other man that you have fallen in love with."

I chuckled at this. "I wish Jesus would return before then."

"So do I, my angel."


Despite my desire to keep a low profile and stay out of the public eye, I continued to go to church in the catacombs. More and more I was convinced through my prayer and meditation that I was doing the right thing.

During that month I spent my time with my studies reading scripture and philosophy. The *Apology of Socrates* was high on my reading list. He was a pagan, but he still died for what he believed was right. I am glad my parents loved me enough to allow me to become educated and an independent thinker. There are so many girls who are taught only what they need to know to function in society.

I would have hated to be like them. I would not have wanted to walk around day by day only doing what I was told and not knowing why. Ignorance is like being blind. I am so glad I can see.

My mother must have felt the way Mary did when Jesus was crucified. She probably felt helpless knowing that I had made up my mind. I understood her pain. Someone had to stand up for what is right. I was only a girl and not very valuable to my family if anything happened to me. They would be sad, but I had to do as my conscience told me.

I hoped my father understood. I thought he did. I didn't know what he would do if I was ever arrested. I probably needed to talk to him again. I didn't want him to come to any harm on my account. Peter denied the Christ; but if he hadn't, he may not have ever gone on to his missionary work and brought the Gospel to Rome in the first place.

# 6

The month of January arrived. I would be celebrating my twelfth birthday. One day there was a knock at our door. My heart fluttered because I had an idea as to who was there. A slave came to my father and told us that Marcus was here to see me. I looked at Father. He nodded to me to give me permission to see him.

He was alone in the atrium. He was so handsome. The Roman world would have wanted us to be together. At that moment I was truly tempted change my mind and to what society wanted for me. However, I needed to remain independent and be with Christ. Marcus had a stern look on his face. His father had not changed his mind.

"You are so beautiful, Agnes," he began without any formal greeting.

"I was thinking the same thing about you."

Marcus then pleaded with me, "Agnes, please marry me." The look on his face was desperate. I could hear in his voice that he truly cared what happened to me.

"You know that I won't."

"My father has been raving for a month about the insult you have given me. He vows that he will humiliate you publicly if you don't."

"You are such a good friend to me, but I mustn't betray my True Love. No humiliation or pain that I would suffer could compare to that which Jesus has already endured for my sake."

"If you married me, I would allow you to continue to worship your God as your household god. I could protect you."

"If you allowed that, you would only put yourself into more danger. Your father might even say that you are a Christian too. Everyone will know where my stance is."

"Not if you continue to worship in secret."

"Should I have to worship in secret?"

"What has this Jesus done for you that you would die for him? You would die for a dead man?"

"Marcus, He is <u>not</u> dead. He lives in me. He lives in all of us who follow Him. He has given me more to live for than those statues or festivals ever could. He has given me hope that there is more to life than appeasing spirits and trying to figure out what they want based on how a chicken eats or whether a calf's liver is the right shape. He gives us freedom to love one another as I love you."

"If you do love me, then marry me. I really want to know more about this Jesus you are so passionate about."

"I'm sorry. I cannot marry you. I have turned my back on everything I used to hold dear. I have made the choice to not marry, so I can remain pure and close to Jesus. I appreciate that you would risk your life for my sake, but I must walk this road with Jesus alone."

"I don't understand you."

"Understand that by law they shouldn't touch me because I am a virgin. I must remain so for my protection. It is my last line of defense against the authorities. Also, remember that whatever they do to my body, they cannot touch my soul. It belongs to Christ; and when He comes again, I will receive a glorified new body. Do not fear for me. I am in good hands."

"Since you won't do what any sane person will do, I need to warn you. My father has publicly denounced you as a Christian. The authorities are coming for you."

There was a loud knock at the door. "They didn't waste any time," he said sadly. "I need to leave. It will be suspicious if I am seen here with you."

"Come with me." I led him toward the back of the house. The knock became persistent. I motioned for a slave to answer the door.

"Wait here in this room until they have gone."

"Stay with me until they call for you."

I heard my father approaching. He called for me, "Agnes!... Agnes!" His voice sounded angry yet frightened. "Where are you child?"

"I am here, Father." I stepped out into the main room.

"I have been looking everywhere for you!" Then softly, he said, "Agnes, there are centurions in the atrium. They are here to arrest you."

"I tried to convince her to marry me to avoid all of this," said Marcus.

"I appreciate your efforts, Marcus, but there is nothing we can do to convince her. Her mind is made up."

From the atrium, the centurion shouted, "We are growing impatient."

"We are coming," replied my father.

Marcus grabbed my hands and looked pleadingly into my eyes. "Please, Agnes."

"May the peace of Christ be with you." This would be the last time that he would see me alone. I removed my hands from his and turned to go. As I went into the atrium, the guards towered above me dwarfing me in their armor with their swords. Yet, I was filled with a power that was beyond me. Every step I made was with confidence.

The centurions seized me and tied my hands behind my back. My father rushed in and asked, "Where are you taking her?"

"To the governor." They took my arms and led me out into the street.

Maximum was standing there waiting for us. He said, "If you will not marry my son, you will marry no one."

"I forgive you. I know you don't understand."

"I spit on your forgiveness. You will not get away with insulting my son." He then addressed the crowd that had gathered. "This girl refused the hand of my son in marriage. He tells me that she considers herself to already have been married to Jesus Christ.

"She is a Christian and a traitor to Rome. I gave her an opportunity to reconsider. I asked to see the person she was married to, but she refuses to produce him. The penalty for treason is death."

"I am a virgin. Your laws cannot execute me."

"You will fulfill your duty to Rome - one way or another."

7

The centurions led me through the streets to the governor. Crowds would stop and look. Some shouted at me. Some asked why they were arresting a child. The sun was bright, but the wind had a cold bite to it. My bonds also began to chafe at my wrists.

When we arrived at our destination, I was led to a huge room. The governor was seated at the opposite end. The centurions led me to the base of the dais. He asked, "Why is this child, a girl, being brought before me?"

Maximum stepped out from behind the entourage and said, "I am Prefect Maximum Herculeus, governor. This girl is a Christian, a traitor to Rome."

"How do you know this?"

"She refuses to marry my son, Marcus."

"What reason does she give?"

"She says that she is dedicating her life to following Jesus of Nazareth. She says that she is married to him."

A flicker of amusement wafted across the governor's face. Then his eyes bored into mine. "What is your name, child?"

"Agnes."

"Is what the prefect says true?"

"Yes, your honor."

"Do you know the punishment for conviction as a Christian?"

"Yes. It is death. I should be executed."

Silence fell upon the room like thunder after my small but determined voice answered this last question. "Maximum, please approach me so we can speak quietly." He went up to the governor and an animated conversation ensued. Words like "traitor" and "virgin" and "against the law" and "punishment" were the few snippets the rest of the audience could understand. When Maximum turned around to go back to where he was standing originally, he had a very angry and disappointed look on his face. This made me happy. It probably meant that my life had been spared.

The governor then turned to me. "Agnes, you must repent from your belief in Jesus. You must worship the gods of Rome. I have decided that since you are a virgin, we cannot lawfully put you to death. We will spare your life. However, you must go to the temple of Minerva to offer an appropriate sacrifice to her on behalf of the state to make up for the fact that you have not been worshipping the way a child of Rome should.

"Centurions, escort her to the temple of Minerva. Maximum, ensure that she offers the sacrifice. Report back to me when she has done so."

The centurions again grasped my upper arms and escorted me out into the street. It was not far to the temple of Minerva. I walked up the steps to the altar. There was a sacrifice there ready for me.

Sacrifices were very important to the Romans. They believed that if a sacrifice was performed incorrectly, bad things would happen. The gods would not appreciate a bad sacrifice and would withhold rain, cause military defeat, or even infertility.

What should I do? Should I just refuse to make the sacrifice? Should I desecrate the sacrifice by pushing it off the altar? I prayed in my heart, "Dear Lord, help me to make the right decision. Your Son's sacrifice is the only one I need or recognize."

Marcus called to me from the street. "Please, Agnes, do the right thing."

As I turned my back to the altar and sat down on the steps, I said, "Don't worry, Marcus. I am doing the right thing."

Maximum spoke up, "Traitor! The girl is a traitor. Look at her refusing to make her prescribed sacrifice."

I stood up and began to walk down to the centurions who had

escorted me to the temple. "My God has already made the ultimate sacrifice. There is no other sacrifice that can be made to save anyone from their sins. Jesus did that for all of us. He..."

At that moment Maximum screamed, "Blasphemy! She speaks lies. Shut her mouth before the gods punish us all."

A centurion clasped me by the arms and placed his hand over my mouth to keep me from speaking the Truth. The other centurion looked at Maximum and told him, "We must return her to the governor since she refused to make the sacrifice."

Therefore, they escorted me back to the governor. As we went back into the courtroom, the he stood up and asked, "Did she complete the sacrifice?"

Maximum replied, "No. She began to spout blasphemy about how there is no sacrifice that is worth anything anymore."

The governor had a puzzled look on his face. "Child, do you know what this means?"

"Yes. I am a traitor and deserve to be put to death." I smiled to myself. We were at an impasse. We both knew that execution was not an option since I was a virgin.

"I will be back later to let you know what I have decided to do about her." He snapped at his advisors, and they followed him out of the room.

I wished that my father could have been there with me, but it wasn't safe for him. This was not his fight anyway. The governor was conferring with his advisors to help him decide what to do with me since I had forced his hand.

After about an hour, the governor returned. He had a very sour look on his face. He glowered at me. Out of respect for his position, I did my best not to smile because he wanted to be taken seriously. "I have made my decision. You refused to make a sacrifice to Minerva. I cannot put you to death since you are a virgin. Therefore, you will sacrifice your body for the state in a brothel."

A look of shock crossed my face. The exact thing I was trying to avoid by not getting married was going to be forced upon me. He was going to force me to lose my virginity so that he would be guiltless when he put me to death.

They took me to a brothel adjacent to one of Rome's circuses. I prayed the whole way there. Jesus was watching over me. No harm would come to me. I was filled with peace.

8

Again, the centurions clasped me by the arms and escorted me from the courtroom. Maximum led a procession that had become a frequent sight that day. I was taken to the brothel by the circus.

Maximum and one of the soldiers led me inside. The leers I received from the men standing in the vestibule were a bit disconcerting. I said a prayer to Jesus. He was with me. Maximum announced to the room, "Here is a treat for you men. She is a virgin and fresh. Any one of you, or as many as would like, may take her to bed."

"She is a lovely child," said one man who was hidden by shadow. I kept my eyes closed and remained in prayer. Someone walked up in front of me. The cool iron of a blade brought chill bumps up on my neck. The dagger cut the collar of my tunic. Someone untied my belt and tore my clothes in two down the front. My body was only covered with my hair which had not been styled or braided that day.

Men in the room made vulgar grunting, moaning sounds. I continued to pray for the protection of the Father, the Son, and the Holy Spirit. A warmth surrounded me. I knew. I knew without a doubt that in this pit of what could have been despair and hopelessness that I would be safe.

There was a presence in front of me that was not divine. I opened my eyes and looked up into the face of a man who had cruel intentions. He moved to grasp me by the shoulders. At that moment the man who moved to touch me was struck blind. A bolt of lightning had struck through the roof of the building. All men who were in direct vicinity of me were singed. The man who tried to touch me was burned very badly.

He screamed and writhed in pain. Finally, he cried out like a small child, "I cannot see. I cannot see! What happened?"

As I looked around the room, the rest of the men, including Maximum were reeling in fear and consternation. Then, Maximum gained some courage. He cried out to those present, "She is a witch! She is calling upon her god to bring destruction upon us!"

Maximum told the centurion to take me out of the brothel and put me in jail. The soldier looked at him and then looked back at me. I finally spoke, "Do not worry. No harm will come to you if you mean no harm to me." The centurion reached down and gave me my tunic. Once my modesty had been reestablished, I reached down and placed my hand over the eyes of the man who had attempted to lay hands on me.

I prayed, "Dear Lord, Jesus, I pray for forgiveness for this man. May your grace flow through me and heal the blindness of this poor soul."

After a few moments, the man opened his eyes and looked up at me. He was at peace. I said, "You have been forgiven. Now, go from this place and sin no more. God bless you."

He reached up and touched my face. He said, "You are an angel from heaven. You are glowing."

"What you see is love. It is the love of Jesus who died for you and for me." He rose from the floor and left.

At this point Maximum was furious. "Seize her!" The centurions grabbed me. I was again taken before the governor.

As I was brought into the court, I could see the frustration in the governor's face. "You have returned, Maximum. Why have you brought her back before me?"

"She is a conundrum. We took her to the brothel to take care of the technicality that is keeping us from executing her."

"What happened?"

"She is a sorceress. She cast a spell on one of the men and struck him blind. Then, she healed him in the name of Jesus."

45

"Is she still a virgin?"

"Yes, Gaius, she is."

"Agnes, we have given you every opportunity to save yourself and demonstrate your loyalty to Rome. You are a traitor. You should die, and you will. I am tired of dealing with you.

"I am sentencing you to die. You shall be burned at the stake. I will also supervise your execution myself since the prefect has been unsuccessful so far.

"This is your last chance. Renounce your god, accept Jupiter and Minerva, or suffer a fiery death."

I stood by myself in front of the governor. Yet, I wasn't alone. I turned to my left, and Marcus was standing there behind a group of people. The look on his face was pleading. I felt so sorry for him since I was the reason for the anguish he was feeling. Christ was with me as well. I could feel Him standing behind me with His hand on my shoulder.

Again, I wished that my father and mother could have been there with me. I understood why they couldn't. My parents didn't deserve to be punished for my decisions. The governor was right that I didn't have to die, but I was not going to allow anyone to tell me how or who to worship. I loved my Jesus. His message is one of love and freedom. He was the sacrifice. He died so that I could live.

I now had the choice of living in bondage to false gods that required blood and appeasement or dying a free woman of my own free will. I had made my choice long ago, but now it was time to stand by it.

"I choose fire." I looked back to where Marcus had been standing. I caught a glimpse of his back as he fled from the room.

"So be it. Place her in chains until a bier can be built for her."

The centurions put me in irons, as if I would run. They threw me into a cell to await my fate.

# 9

The next morning the guards came to my cell after the sun had risen. I had slept well after I spent several hours in prayer. I was ready. They escorted me from the cell out into the cold January morning. The day was bright and sunny. The sky was a beautiful, azure blue. A peace filled me. I was ready.

I was chained to a stake wearing a clean tunic that my mother had sent. It was brought anonymously, but I could smell her on the fabric. Wood was stacked around my feet. It was dry, so it should light and burn quickly.

The governor and Maximum stood before me and addressed the crowd that had gathered expectantly to witness my death. Maximum spoke first, "This woman is a traitor to Rome. She has refused to marry my son, Marcus. She has refused because she says she is married to Jesus Christ.

"The last I knew this Christ was put to death nearly three hundred years ago. Therefore, she is a liar as well as a Christian.

"She is also a sorceress. She struck a man blind and then healed him in the name of Jesus yesterday."

A brave voice from the crowd spoke up, "She is a virgin! It is against the law to execute her."

The governor then spoke up. "She is a traitor to Rome. She has refused numerous opportunities to show her allegiance to Her. She must be executed to set an example to all traitors. They must know that Rome will not be betrayed.

"Neither she nor any other Christian will be able to hide behind any status to avoid the penalty of death.

"It is time. Light the fire."

The executioner took a torch and shoved it deeply into the pyre. The kindling ignited and flames began to rise up around my feet. It was warm but not hot. I could feel the flames, but I did not burn. Something or someone was protecting me.

I could hear the crowd crying out in amazement. Several of them shouted, "They cannot execute a virgin."

"Her God is protecting her."

"It's a miracle!"

"I can see Jesus standing with her!"

It was this last comment that ended my burning at the stake. The governor hurriedly ordered the executioner and his guards to put out the fire.

The crowd was silent. The Roman officials were seething. The governor and Maximum looked at each other. I was at peace because God was with me.

The governor spoke to a centurion that was near him who immediately went away as if to run an errand. Once the fire was out, the guards that had been with me all of the previous day took hold of me yet again. I was untied from the stake and brought down before the governor for the last time. The centurion who had been sent away came back with a large block of wood and another man with a hood over his head carried a sword.

"This girl is obviously a sorceress who calls on the powers of non-Roman gods. She is a traitor and must be put to death. Since flames cannot harm her, she will be beheaded."

The guards moved me to the block. I knelt down and placed my head upon it. There were several cries of protest from the crowd. Many were decrying the decision to execute a virgin. Others shamed Maximum that his pride would lead to this. "You shall not have died in vain, Agnes," another member of the crowd shouted.

With no further ceremony, the executioner took his sword, brought it down on my neck, and severed my head from my body.

\*\*\*

Fortunately, this is not where my story ends. The people of Rome were appalled at my execution. I was innocent in their eyes; and because of this, the authorities allowed my parents to bury me in their cemetery. Many people began to inquire of the faith that I had professed and had given me such courage in the face of cruelty and evil. The Church of Rome grew greatly after my death, and I became one of the best known of the martyrs of that time.

The next year on the anniversary of my birthday my parents went to visit my grave. They saw a vision of me surrounded by virgins in heaven with a white lamb by my side. Now every year on my feast day lambs are presented at the church that was constructed over my tomb. The lambs are sheared and stoles are woven for the archbishops of the Roman Catholic Church from their wool.

Over the next several years the Roman Empire fell apart. The western half of the empire fell into neglect and barbarian tribes from the north invaded and sacked Rome. The government had more important things to worry about than Christians and who and how they worshipped. The year following my death, Diocletian resigned as emperor of the western half of the empire, and after several months of political wrangling, Constantine was made emperor.

Shortly after my death the people of Rome had become much more tolerant of Christians, and Christians began to be able to practice openly again. The survival of Christianity at that time was guaranteed when Constantine had his vision of a cross in the sky before the Battle of the Milvian Bridge in A.D. 312 against a pretender to the Roman throne, Maximian. Constantine had his soldiers paint red crosses on their shields and promised God that if he won the battle, he would become a follower of Christ. He did win and became the first Christian emperor of Rome.

My name is still mentioned in prayers of the Roman Catholic Church which praise me for my courage in the face of adversity. I hope that my story will give others courage to face authority that might threaten freedom to practice our faith.

Remember that God will always be with you, Jesus will always protect you, and the Holy Spirit will always guide you in the right. May the blessings of Christ be upon you all the days of your life. Amen.

# BIBLIOGRAPHY

Cowell, F.R. *Everyday Life in Ancient Rome.* New York: G.P. Putnam's Sons, 1961.

Fremantle, Anne. *A Treasury of Early Christianity.* New York: New American Library, 1953.

Hadas, Moses. *Imperial Rome.* New York: Time, Inc, 1965.

Lyttelton, Margaret and Werner Forman. *The Romans: Their Gods and Their Beliefs.* London: Orbis Publishing Ltd., 1984.

Keyes, Frances Parkinson. "Agnes of Rome." *Three Ways of Love.* New York: Hawthorn Books, Inc., 1963.

Payne, Robert, ed. *Horizon Book of Ancient Rome.* New York: American Heritage Publishing Co., Inc., 1966.

World Bible Publishing. *God's Word: Today's Bible Translation That Says What It Means.* God's Word Series, 1995.

# ABOUT THE AUTHOR

Catherine Brigden was born in Texas where her heart resides. She graduated from the University of Dallas. She is a former teacher who now works with her husband in rural Oklahoma. She has two teenage children: one in college and one in high school.

Her true love is her lord and savior Jesus Christ, and she prays that all who read this book will come to know Him better.

"Jesus did many other things as well. If every one of them were written down, I suppose that even the whole world would not have room for the books that would be written." – John 21:35 NIV

Made in the USA
Lexington, KY
16 November 2016